Dirty Bertie
BOGEYS!

D0587215

For Lynsey ~ D R

For Olivia and Natasha –

with best Berties ~ A M

STRIPES PUBLISHING
An imprint of Little Tiger Press
1 The Coda Centre, 189 Munster Road,
London SW6 6AW

A paperback original
First published in Great Britain in 2009

Characters created by David Roberts
Text copyright © Alan MacDonald, 2009
Illustrations copyright © David Roberts, 2009

ISBN: 978-1-84715-071-4

Printed and bound in the UK.

10 9 8 7

Dirty Bertie

BOGEYS!

DAVID ROBERTS WRITTEN BY ALAN MACDONALD

Stripes

Collect all the Dirty Bertie books!

Contents

CHAPTER 1

"BERTIE!" Miss Boot thundered. "ARE YOU PAYING ATTENTION?"

Bertie shot upright.

CRACK!

"OW!" He had forgotten he was looking for his rubber under his desk. He peeped out, rubbing his head.

"SIT DOWN!" barked Miss Boot.

"Now what was I just saying?"

"When?" asked Bertie.

"While you were crawling around under your desk."

Bertie racked his brains trying to remember. The truth was he hadn't been following too closely. Whenever Miss Boot started talking, Bertie's mind had a habit of wandering off.

"Um, you were saying…" Bertie looked to Eugene for help. Eugene mouthed something he didn't quite catch.

"You were saying … about fried eggs."

The class sniggered. Eugene whispered in his ear.

"Oh, *Friday*. You were saying about Friday."

Miss Boot folded her arms. "Yes, and

what's happening on Friday? Do tell us."

Bertie hadn't the faintest clue. "We're having a day off?" he said, hopefully.

More laughter.

THUMP! Miss Boot's fist slammed down on her desk.

"We are *not* having a day off. I was talking about our visitor. Can anyone tell Bertie who's coming to school on Friday?"

Dirty Bertie

A sea of hands rose in the air. Miss Boot's eyes fell on the pale boy bouncing up and down in the front row like an eager puppy.

"Yes, Nicholas?"

"The Mayoress," said Know-All Nick.

"Quite right. I'm glad *someone* is paying attention," said Miss Boot.

Nick smirked at Bertie. Bertie scowled back.

Miss Boot went on. "It's a great honour to have someone as important as the Mayoress coming to our school. I'm sure you're all very excited."

Bertie yawned. Why were school visitors always so boring? Why didn't they invite someone interesting for a change — like a lion tamer or a brain surgeon?

"Now," said Miss Boot, eyeing the class,

Dirty Bertie

"Miss Skinner would like one of our class to do a special job. One lucky child is going to welcome the Mayoress in assembly. Who wants to volunteer?"

The hands shot up again. Bertie couldn't see what all the fuss was about. Know-All Nick was jiggling around as if he needed the toilet.

"Ooh, Miss, Miss! Me, me!" he gasped.

Dirty Bertie

Miss Boot hesitated. Last time there was a visitor she had chosen Nick to meet them. And the time before.

"Hands down," she said. "Since so many of you are keen, we will put all your names in a hat and draw one out."

Everyone wrote their name on a piece of paper and put it in a biscuit tin. (Miss Boot didn't actually have a hat.) Miss Boot drew out one scrap of paper and unfolded it. She read the name scrawled in big letters. She turned white. She looked as if she might pass out.

"Who? Who is it?" everyone asked.

"Bertie," groaned Miss Boot.

Bertie looked up from doodling on his maths book.

"What? I wasn't doing anything," he said.

Miss Boot sighed. "If you were listening, Bertie, you'd know that you've been chosen to welcome the Mayoress."

"ME?" said Bertie. "*Really?*"

"Really," said Miss Boot. The bell went for break. She screwed up the piece of paper in her hand. She needed to find somewhere quiet to lie down.

CHAPTER 2

"*You?*" said Dad.

"*You?*" said Suzy. "They want *you* to meet the Mayor?"

"Actually, it's the Mayor-hess," Bertie said.

"But why *you?*" asked Suzy. "They had the whole school to choose from! Why didn't they pick someone with half a brain?"

Bertie ignored this remark. "Miss Boot thought I'd be good at it," he said. "Meeting mayor-hesses and that. Making speeches."

Dad looked horrified. "Surely they don't want you to make a speech?"

"I don't know yet," said Bertie. "We're having a practice on Thursday."

Mum put an arm round his shoulder. "Well, I think it's wonderful, Bertie," she said. "I'm very proud of you."

"Yes," said Bertie, sticking out his tongue at his sister. He hadn't mentioned that he had been selected by pure chance. It was a small detail.

Suzy still couldn't believe it. "Has your teacher got a screw loose?" she asked. "Does she *know* what you're like?"

"I don't see why you're making such a fuss," said Bertie. "All I've got to do is give her a bunch of old flowers. It's not difficult."

"Of course it's not," said Mum. "But it is the Mayoress and she is very important…"

"*I've* never heard of her," said Bertie.

"…And the whole school will be watching," Mum went on.

"Oh yes, I forgot," said Bertie. "Miss Boot says a man from the *Pudsley Post* is coming as well."

"The newspaper?"

"Yes, he's going to take my picture with the Mayor-hess."

"Good heavens! Is that a good idea?" asked Dad.

Bertie frowned. He'd expected a bit more enthusiasm. He thought his family would be *pleased* that his picture was going to be in the paper.

"I'm sure it will all be fine," said Mum. "Just as long as you don't do anything … silly."

"Like what?" asked Bertie.

"Burping," said Suzy.

"Or talking with your mouth full," said Dad.

"And *please, please, please*, Bertie, don't pick your nose," pleaded Mum.

"I won't," said Bertie. "When do I pick my nose?"

"Only every five minutes," said Suzy, scornfully.

Dirty Bertie

"Well, what does it matter? It's *my* nose," said Bertie. "It's not as if I go round picking any old nose!"

Mum rolled her eyes. "You just cannot do it. Not when you're meeting the Mayoress."

"I won't!"

"Or the other thing," said Suzy.

"What other thing?"

"You know – eating bogeys!" said Suzy. "It's disgusting!"

Dirty Bertie

"I don't!"

"You do!"

Dad held up a hand. "In any case, nose picking is a horrible habit and it's time you gave it up," he said.

"I will," said Bertie. "But…"

"No buts," said Mum, firmly. "I want you to promise."

Bertie sighed heavily. "I promise," he said. "You won't catch me picking my nose again."

CHAPTER 3

Bertie went upstairs to his room, humming to himself. He'd promised his parents they wouldn't *catch* him picking his nose – so he'd just have to make sure he wasn't caught.

In any case, he didn't see what all the fuss was about. Everyone picked their nose. His friends certainly did. Bertie and

Dirty Bertie

Darren often compared bogeys to see who had the biggest. They'd invented several bogey games, including Bogey Golf, Bogey Table Football and Roller-Bogey.

Grown-ups picked their noses, too. Bertie had seen his dad do it when he was driving. And Miss Boot did it when she was reading a book. He bet even the Queen picked her nose when no one was looking.

So what was the harm if Bertie sometimes had a good clean out? Talking of which, there was no one about now…

"BERTIE!" Mum stuck her head round the door. "Remember what you promised!"

"I wasn't!" cried Bertie. "I just had an itch."

Mum tutted. "I'm watching you."

Bertie flopped down on his bed. This was terrible. If you couldn't pick your nose in your own bedroom where could you do it?

Five minutes later, he slipped out of the back door. His Top Secret Hideout was behind the garden shed. Darren and Eugene were the only ones who knew about it and they were sworn to secrecy.

Dirty Bertie

Bertie pushed his way in among the
bushes and sat down. Alone at last.
Now for…

"BERTIE! What are you doing?"

Dad was staring at him through the
shed window.

"Nothing!" said Bertie. "I was just looking for Whiffer."

"He's asleep on the sofa. Come out of there! It's filthy!"

Bertie drooped back to the house. This was hopeless. His parents wouldn't leave him alone for five minutes. He was actually glad when it was time to go to bed.

Mum came up to tuck him in.

"Goodnight, Bertie!"

"Night, Mum."

"Sleep tight!"

CLICK! Off went the bedroom light. Peace and quiet at last. No one to disturb him. Bliss. Bertie's finger crept out from under the covers.

"BERTIE!" called Mum. "STOP PICKING YOUR NOSE!"

Dirty Bertie

CHAPTER 4

For the rest of the week, Bertie's parents
watched him like vultures. He couldn't
even lift a hand without Mum tutting or
Dad glaring at him. He tried to find
places where he could be by himself.
On Tuesday Mum found him hiding in
the towel cupboard. On Wednesday
Dad caught him in Whiffer's kennel.

Dirty Bertie

School was just as bad. Miss Boot
made him practise his part for assembly
over and over again. She barked orders
at him: "Don't slouch! Hands out of your
pockets! Stop mumbling – SPEAK UP!"

Dirty Bertie

By the time Friday came round Bertie
was beginning to wish he'd never been
chosen. He wished he was sitting with
his friends instead of standing at the
front with a bunch of droopy flowers.
He could see Darren and Eugene pulling
faces at him. Darren put two fingers up
his nose as a joke.

Dirty Bertie

The man from the *Pudsley Post* was ready with his camera. Bertie shuffled his feet nervously. What if he did something wrong? What if he tripped on the steps? Or trod on the flowers? What if he forgot what to say?

The hall was hot and airless. Miss Boot was frowning at him. More than anything Bertie was *dying* to pick his nose. He always picked his nose when he was nervous and now it was like having a terrible itch which you couldn't scratch.

Dirty Bertie

His nose felt bunged up. He was convinced he had a giant bogey poking out of one nostril. But he didn't dare investigate – not with the whole school watching.

A door opened and Miss Skinner entered, followed by the Mayoress.

Bertie had been expecting someone royal like the Queen. But the Mayoress could have been one of his gran's friends.

 She wore a plum-coloured dress, which matched her face. Round her neck was a large silver chain.

She took a seat while Miss Skinner turned to face the rows of children.

"We are extremely honoured – blah blah blah," droned Miss Skinner.

Bertie had stopped listening. He'd just noticed no one in the hall was looking at him. They were all gazing up at the Mayoress and her silver chain.

Go on, said a voice in Bertie's head. *One little pick. What harm can it do?* Bertie bent his head as if he needed to scratch his nose. It didn't take more than a few seconds.

"BERTIE!" hissed Miss Boot. *"Hurry up! We're waiting!"*

Bertie dropped his hand. Had he been spotted? He glanced round – no, but Miss Skinner had stopped talking. Everyone was waiting for him to welcome the visitor. He thudded up the steps and on to the stage. He thrust the droopy flowers at the Mayoress.

"For-you-Miss-Mayor-hess-from-all-the-children," he gabbled in one breath.

"Oh! Thank you. How kind," smiled the Mayoress.

Bertie turned away. Everything might have been all right if he'd gone back to his place there and then. But he realized he'd forgotten something. He was meant to shake hands. He turned back and stuck out one sweaty hand. Bertie stared in horror. There was something stuck to the end of his finger: a giant green bogey.

The Mayoress had seen it, too. She bent closer to examine it.

"Oh! What is that?"

Dirty Bertie

"What?" asked Bertie.

"That *thing* stuck to your finger."

"Oh, er, that," said Bertie. "It's um … it's a…"

And then he did it. The thing he claimed he never did. The thing that no one in the school who saw it happen would ever forget. The thing you must *never* do when someone is about to take your picture for the paper…

CHAPTER 1

"Bagsy sit at the back!"

Bertie clattered up the steps on to the coach. It was the day of the school trip. Bertie loved going on trips. He loved the coach ride there, the packed lunches and pulling faces at passing cars. He loved drawing on the windows, stuffing crisps and fizzy drinks – and being sick on the way home. Best of all, a trip meant a whole day without boring lessons. No mouldy maths or dreary spelling! No hours of listening to Miss Boot droning on and on.

Today the class were going to Rustbottom Hall. Miss Boot said it was an Historic Building, hundreds of years old. Bertie couldn't wait. Last year, Darren's family had been to Cannonshot Castle. It had a moat and battlements and a headless ghost in the West Tower. There was even something called a joust, where real knights in armour fought each other on horseback. Bertie thought he'd make a brilliant knight. Sir Bertie of the Green Bogey. He would rescue princesses and slay fire-breathing dragons – Miss Boot had better watch out.

Bertie raced to the back
seat, only to find Know-All Nick and his
weedy pal, Trevor, had got there first.
They were sucking sherbet lemons.
Handing out sweets was the only way
Nick could get anyone to sit next to him.

Dirty Bertie

"Too slow, Bertie," smirked Nick.

Bertie scowled and sat down next to Darren in the seats in front.

DOINK!

Something hit Bertie on the head and bounced off. He turned round.

Dirty Bertie

"Did you throw that?"

"Throw what?" Nick gave him a sickly smile.

Bertie picked a yellow sweet off the floor. "This!"

"I don't know what you're talking about," sneered Nick. "Seen anyone throwing sweets, Trevor?"

"Er, no, Nick," said Trevor meekly.

"Liar," said Bertie.

"Frogface," replied Nick.

"Yeah, frogface," said Trevor.

"You wait…" said Bertie.

"BERTIE! I WON'T TELL YOU AGAIN! TURN ROUND!" thundered Miss Boot.

"But Miss, it wasn't me…"

"SIT DOWN! And if I see you turn round again, you will sit next to me."

41

Dirty Bertie

Bertie flopped back into his seat. He didn't want to sit next to Miss Boot. He'd rather sit in a bath of cold custard. All the same, he would get even with that sneaky know-all. Maybe Rustbottom Hall had a deep, dark dungeon? Maybe he could lock the door and leave Nick to the rats.

CHAPTER 2

The coach swung into the drive and
came to a halt. Bertie trooped off with
the rest of the class, eager to start
exploring. He stared. Rustbottom Hall
was a crumbly old house with a clock
tower and a wonky weather vane. The
roof was whitewashed with pigeon poo.

"*Is this it?*" asked Bertie.

Dirty Bertie

"Isn't it magnificent?" said Miss Boot.
"This hall has been home to the
Rustbottom family since the 17th century."

"But where's the moat?" asked Bertie.

"There isn't a moat."

"And where's the drawbridge?"

"It has a front door."

"But where are the
knights going to do the
jousting?"

Miss Boot gave
Bertie a pained look.
"Rustbottom
Hall is not
a castle,"
she
snapped.
"It is a
house."

Dirty Bertie

A *house*? Bertie couldn't believe it. He'd been looking forward to seeing a real castle. Battling on the battlements. Rampaging round the ramparts. What was the point of coming all this way to see a crumbly old house? If he wanted to see a house he could have stayed at home!

"It's not like Cannonshot Castle," grumbled Darren.

"It's falling to bits," moaned Eugene.

"QUIET!" thundered Miss Boot. "Now, we will be having a short tour of the hall. After that we'll split into groups to do an exciting quiz. Follow me, class."

They trudged inside the hall. It was cold, dark and smelt of mothballs. There were podgy little angels painted on the ceiling.

Dirty Bertie

Dirty Bertie

"Remember," warned Miss Boot, "no running, no noise and you are not to touch anything. Everything in this house is old and very valuable."

Bertie plunged his hands into his pockets. This was the worst school trip ever. They'd had more fun last year at the sewage farm. At least Trevor had slipped and fallen in.

The tour of the house went on for ages. Twice the guide had to ask Bertie not to yawn so loudly. Afterwards, Miss Boot divided them into groups.

Bertie's group had Darren and Eugene (which was good), and Sandra (which was not so good).

"I don't want to be with Bertie,"

sulked Sandra. "I want to go with Lucy."

Miss Boot took no notice. She handed a worksheet to each group. It involved trailing around the hall to answer a list of questions. Bertie stared at it in horror. *Thirty* questions? It would take *days* to answer them all! He felt tired just looking at them.

"I don't have a pencil," he said.

"I told you to bring one," snapped Miss Boot.

Bertie searched his pockets. "I did. I must have lost it."

"Then share with Darren." Miss Boot glared at him. "Work as a group to answer the questions. And Bertie?"

"Yes, Miss?"

"Do *not* touch anything. Not even the door handles."

Dirty Bertie

Bertie trailed after
Darren, Eugene and
Sandra.

"Why can't I be the one
to write the answers?"
grumbled Sandra.

"It's my pencil,"
said Darren.

"Can't I borrow it?"

"No."

"Please?"

"No."

"You're mean and ugly
and I hate you," said Sandra.
"I want to be in Lucy's
group."

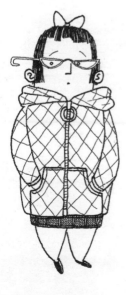

Bertie looked over
Darren's shoulder. "How
many have we done so far?"

Darren checked the sheet. "None."

Know-All Nick breezed past them. He had brought his own pen and clipboard. He was in a group with Trevor, Alice and Mia.

"What's the matter? Stuck already, Bertie?" jeered Nick in his reedy voice.

"No," said Bertie. "We've answered loads."

"How many?"

"Three," lied Bertie.

"We've done four," boasted Nick. "*And* we've got them all right. I bet we get loads more right than you."

Dirty Bertie

Bertie watched them hurry off in search of the next answer. He hated to be beaten at anything by Know-All Nick. He hadn't forgotten the time Nick had taken the part he wanted in the Christmas play. If Nick's team got top marks in the quiz, he would boast about it for weeks. Well, Bertie would show that smarty-pants show-off.

"We've got to beat them," he said. "We can't let them win."

"How?" asked Darren. "They've got all the brainboxes in their group."

"They haven't got me," said Bertie.

"Or me," said Eugene.

"Or me," said Sandra.

"No," said Darren. "Like I said, they've got all the brainboxes."

"How long have we got left?" asked Bertie.

Darren checked his watch. "Um … twenty … thirty … not that long."

"We'll have to speed up," said Bertie, taking charge. "If we whiz round we can find all the answers before them. Where to next?"

Darren checked the sheet. "The library."

CHAPTER 3

They charged along the corridor, with Bertie leading the way.

"How many books are there?" Darren read out.

Bertie looked at the shelves. "Millions."

"Better start counting then," said a sneering voice. Know-All Nick leaned in the doorway.

"We know the answer," he smirked.
"Want us to give you a clue?"

"No. Get lost." Bertie glared.

"It's so easy," said Know-All Nick.

"Yeah, easy-peasy," said Trevor.

"Come on," said Nick to his team.
"Let's leave the dunces to work it out."

Bertie's group charged upstairs. And
downstairs. Up more stairs. Along
corridors. Into broom cupboards. But
however fast they went, Nick's group
always got to the answer before them.

With time running out, they found
themselves on the top floor. Bertie
looked at their sheet. They'd left eight
questions blank and Darren had
doodled on two of them. Bertie didn't

feel that confident about the rest of
their answers either.

Q7: What was the
name of the 5th Lord
Rustbottom's wife?
A: Mrs Rustbottom

Q8: What are a pair of
bellows used for?
A: Shouting

Q9: What is unusual about
the guests' bathroom?
A: It smells of wee

Bertie sighed. There
was no way they were going to win. But
they couldn't just stand by and watch Nick
come top. They had to do something.

"Where are we?" said Eugene.

Bertie read a label on the wall. "The Blue Bedroom. And look, this is the last question: 'What can you see on the chamber pot?'"

"What's a chamber pot?" asked Darren.

Bertie pointed. "Look! By the bed!"

"Ha ha!" giggled Darren. "It's a potty!"

On a cabinet sat a pale-blue potty
with a Chinese pattern.

"Dragons," said Bertie. "That's the
answer. It's got dragons on it!"

"Brilliant!" Darren wrote it down in
the box. "Do you think we're the first
ones here?"

"Looks like it," said Eugene.

Suddenly Bertie had an idea. "Why
don't we hide it?"

"What?" said Eugene.

"The potty. Then Nick's team will
never get the answer."

Sandra stared. "Miss Boot said we
weren't to touch anything."

"She'll never know," said Darren.
"Anyway *we're* not going to touch it.
Bertie will."

"*Me?*" said Bertie.

Darren shrugged. "It's your idea. And I'm doing all the writing, I can't do everything!"

"I'm not touching it," said Eugene, hastily.

"Nor me," said Sandra.

Bertie hesitated. If he got caught he'd be in major trouble. But it would be worth it to see Nick's face when he, Bertie, gave the right answer. He got down on his hands and knees to crawl under the rope barrier.

"Hurry up!" hissed Darren. "Before anyone comes."

"I am hurrying!" Bertie reached out and made a grab for the potty, knocking over a candlestick. It rolled across the cabinet and clattered on to the floor.

A moment later a much louder noise
split the air.

DDDDRRRRRIIIIIINNNG!

Bertie turned pale.

"You've set off the alarm!" gasped
Darren.

"Miss Boot'll kill you," said Eugene.

"Told you so," said Sandra.

Dirty Bertie

Bertie was dancing around with the potty in his hands. "What shall I do?" he cried.

"I don't know!" said Darren. "Hide it!"

Bertie looked around in desperation. He could hear voices approaching. Feet thundering up the stairs. Any moment now they would burst in and he'd be caught. He did the only thing he could think of. He unzipped his jacket and stuffed the potty inside.

CHAPTER 4

Miss Boot's gaze swept over the class like an icy wind.

"Some foolish person has set off the alarm," she said. "I trust *none of you* know anything about it."

The class shook their heads. Bertie tried not to look in Miss Boot's direction. He was sweating. Could she see the big lump under his jacket? How on earth was he going to smuggle the potty back inside without getting caught?

"The staff are checking the house to make sure nothing's missing," said Miss Boot. "So, while we are waiting, let's go through the answers to the quiz."

The class took out their sheets of paper.

"Right," said Miss Boot. "Who can tell me the answer to question one?"

Know-All Nick's hand shot into the air.

Twenty minutes later, Nick's team had scored 28 marks out of 29. Bertie's team had scored two.

"Number 30, last question," boomed

Dirty Bertie

Miss Boot. "In the Blue Bedroom, what can you see on the chamber pot?"

Silence. Only one hand went up. It belonged to Bertie.

Dirty Bertie

"Bertie?" said Miss Boot, surprised.
"You know the answer, do you?"

"Yes, Miss. It's dragons."

"Dragons?" Miss Boot checked her
sheet. "The answer I have is sea monsters."

Bertie was outraged. "No! Dragons."

"I'm sorry, I have sea monsters here."

"But they're dragons, Miss!"

"No arguing, Bertie."

"But Miss, they *are*!"

Miss Boot turned away. "Final scores then."

This was too much. Bertie unzipped his jacket.

"Dragons," he said. "Look, I'll show you!"

He held up the potty for everyone to see. Eugene covered his eyes.

Miss Boot's face turned white, then purple.

"BERTIE," she thundered. "WHERE DID YOU GET THAT?"

"Oh, um … I can explain," mumbled Bertie.

"Bring it here. NOW!" ordered Miss Boot.

Bertie pushed his way through the crowd. Now he was *really* for it. He was so busy worrying about his punishment, that he didn't see Know-All Nick stick out a leg.

Bertie tripped. The potty slipped from his grasp.

CRAAAASH!

There was a shocked silence. Bits of priceless potty littered the grass.

Bertie looked up at Miss Boot.

Dirty Bertie

"Whoops!" he said. "Good job it was only an old one!"

MAGIC!

CHAPTER 1

"A present? For me?"

Bertie tore off the bag and stared at the black, shiny box.

☆ *The Marvo Magic Set* ☆
☆ *Amaze your friends!* ☆

"A magic set?" he gasped.

Gran smiled. "I saw it in a shop window and thought of you. Do you like it?"

Like it? Bertie would have happily swapped his sister for a magic set. He'd always wanted to do magic. He ripped off the lid. Inside were cards, boxes and plastic cups – everything he needed to become a world famous magician. Bertie put on the black cloak and magician's hat. He waved his magic wand.

"Careful!" said Gran. "I don't want you turning me into a toad!"

Bertie stared at her. "You think I'll be able to do *real magic?*" he asked.

"Of course! With a bit of practice."

"Fantastic!" said Bertie.

The set came with the *Marvo Book of 101 Magic Tricks.* It was a fat book with a lot of pages. Bertie didn't have time to read it right now, he wanted to get started on some magic straight away.

Dirty Bertie

"Pick a card, Gran," he said, holding out a pack. Gran took a card.

"Don't let me see it," said Bertie. He screwed up his eyes, frowning hard.

"The King of Hearts!" he said.

"Goodness! So it is!" laughed Gran.

"Really?" said Bertie, amazed.

"Definitely," said Gran. "The King of Hearts. How on earth did you guess?"

"I don't know," said Bertie. "It must be magic!"

Bertie could hardly believe it. *This is fantastic*, he thought. *All these years I had magic powers and I never even knew!*

He rushed into the kitchen.

"Mum! Mum! I can do magic!"

"That's nice," said Mum, sipping her coffee.

"No, listen — real magic! Ask me to make something disappear."

"OK … what about this?" Mum held up a half-eaten chocolate biscuit.

"Watch!" said Bertie.

He closed his eyes and thought magic thoughts. He waved his wand three times. When he opened his eyes, the biscuit had vanished.

"See! I told you! Magic!" he said.

"That's amazing, Bertie!" said Mum, who seemed to have her mouth full.

Dirty Bertie

Bertie was on fire with excitement. He could do anything. He could turn his teachers to stone. He could make sweets grow on trees. He could make his sister his slave. Wait till he told his friends about this!

Dirty Bertie

Half an hour later, Bertie was standing in Eugene's garden.

"What are you going to do?" asked Eugene, nervously.

"Just a magic spell," said Bertie. "I've got to practise on someone."

"Why can't you practise on Darren?"

Darren shook his head. "It's best to start on someone smaller. Why don't you turn him into a spider?"

"No!" cried Eugene. "I don't like spiders!"

"A worm, that'll be easy, he looks like a worm," grinned Darren.

"All right," said Bertie. "Close your eyes."

"Promise it won't hurt?" said Eugene.

"Go on!"

Eugene reluctantly closed his eyes. Bertie covered his head with a black cloth.

"It's dark! I don't like it!" wailed Eugene.

"Keep your eyes closed! That's the magic cloth," said Bertie.

"It's not your hanky, is it? I don't want your germs!"

"Quiet!" said Bertie. "How can I do spells if you keep talking?"

Bertie frowned. He raised his magic wand and chanted the magic words:

Stinky pinky, ponky squirm,
Change Eugene into a worm!

75

He whipped off the magic cloth.

"ARGHH!" screamed Darren.

"What?" gasped Eugene.

"Just your ugly face!" hooted Darren. "Ha ha!"

Bertie couldn't understand it. He'd waved his wand and repeated the spell, so why hadn't it worked? When he'd tried the magic on Mum and Gran it had worked perfectly.

"You opened your eyes," he said.

"It's not my fault," said Eugene. "You must have said it wrong."

"This is boring. Let's do something else," yawned Darren.

"It will work," said Bertie. "I just need a bit more practice."

Just then, Eugene's mum stuck her head out of the back door.

Dirty Bertie

"Bertie!" she called. "Your mum's on the phone!"

Bertie sighed. He pocketed his wand and went inside.

Darren watched him go.

"Hey, Eugene," he said. "Want to play a trick on Bertie?"

"What kind of trick?"

"A magic trick of course."

Eugene frowned. "Do I have to wear a hanky on my head?"

"You don't have to do anything," said Darren. "Listen, this is what we do…"

CHAPTER 2

Five minutes later, Bertie was back. He looked around in surprise.

"Where's Eugene?"

Darren didn't answer. His mouth was open in astonishment.

"L-l-look!" he said.

"What's the matter?"

"There! Look!"

Dirty Bertie

Bertie stared. Eugene's jumper lay on the grass. Something inside it was wriggling around. They both squatted down to take a closer look. A small pink head peeped out of the collar. It was followed by a long pink body.

"See?" gasped Darren. "It worked!"

"What?"

"You did it! You actually turned Eugene into a worm!"

Bertie stared. "*That's* Eugene?"

"It must be!"

"But he was here a minute ago!"

"I know. Then there was a flash of smoke and stuff – and the next minute he'd gone!"

Bertie stared at the tiny wriggling worm. "You're sure that's *him*?"

"Of course! That's his jumper, isn't it?"

"Wow!" said Bertie. "I did it! I actually did it! I told you I could do magic!"

The worm was wriggling its way across Eugene's jumper, trying to escape. Bertie picked it up, letting it wriggle on the palm of his hand. It was slimy and cold to the touch.

Bertie could see now that it was definitely Eugene. It had the same worried expression.

Dirty Bertie

"Careful," said Darren. "Don't drop him!"

Bertie cupped Eugene in both hands so he couldn't escape. This was incredible. Astonishing. He – the Amazing Bertie – had actually turned Eugene into a weeny wiggling worm. If he could do this, there was no limit to his magic powers. People would pay millions just to come and watch him perform…

"No hurry," said Darren, "but hadn't you better change him back?"

"What?"

"Change him back. You can't leave him like that. A blackbird might eat him."

81

Dirty Bertie

Bertie hadn't thought of that. Still, it shouldn't be that difficult for a master magician. If he could turn Eugene into a worm, changing him back would be a piece of cake. He set Eugene down and covered him with the magic cloth. He raised his wand and waved it three times in the air.

Biggly boggly, bogeys green,
Turn this worm into Eugene!

Bertie whipped off the magic cloth. The worm raised its head – or maybe its bottom, it was hard to tell. Bertie twiddled his wand.

"Um … maybe we just need to wait a few minutes," he said.

CHAPTER 3

The minutes ticked by. They were still staring at the worm on the grass.

"This is not good," said Darren. "This is a disaster. This is a—"

"Yes, OK, don't go on!" snapped Bertie.

He couldn't understand it. The spell had worked fine the first time, so what had gone wrong? Maybe he'd waved his wand

too often or muddled the magic words.
He tried the spell again – and again.
Nothing happened. This was terrible. He'd
changed Eugene into a wiggling worm
and now he couldn't bring him back!

"What are we going to do?" he asked.

"Don't ask me," said Darren. "You're
the magician!"

"It'll probably wear off," said Bertie,
hopefully. "Spells don't last for ever, do
they?"

"What if it doesn't?" said Darren.
"What are you going to tell Eugene's
mum? She'll go potty!"

"Shut up!" said Bertie. "I just need to
think." He was pacing up and down the
lawn. Maybe he should take Eugene home
with him and consult his *Marvo Book of
101 Magic Tricks*?

Dirty Bertie

"EUGENE! Your supper's ready!"

Bertie froze in horror. Eugene's mum was coming down the path towards them.

"Quick – hide him!" hissed Darren.

Bertie scooped up Eugene and slipped him into his pocket.

Eugene's mum stopped and gave them a puzzled look.

"Where's Eugene? I thought he was with you?"

"No," said Bertie. "He … um … he went in to change."

"Change?"

"Yes, to change into something smaller," said Darren, grinning.

Bertie gave him a sharp kick. Eugene's mum was looking at them as if they were up to something.

"That's odd. I didn't see him come in," she said.

"Didn't you?" said Bertie. "Maybe he just sneaked past."

"Yes, probably *wormed* his way in," said Darren.

Bertie shot him a warning look. "Anyway," he said, "we've got to be going, haven't we, Darren?"

Dirty Bertie

"Have we?"

"Yes. You know, my mum said I've got to go home…"

"URRGHHH!"

Eugene's mum had suddenly leaped backwards, as if she'd stepped in something nasty.

Bertie looked down and saw the worm dangling from his pocket. He was wriggling around, trying to escape. Bertie quickly pushed him back in.

Dirty Bertie

"There's a worm in your pocket!" screeched Eugene's mum.

"Yes, he's my pet worm," said Bertie. "He likes it in there."

"Bertie calls him Eugene, don't you, Bertie?" said Darren.

"Um … yes," said Bertie, turning red. "Although he's not Eugene, obviously. He's just a worm. Anyway, we better be going…"

He backed away and fled up the garden path.

CHAPTER 4

Back home, Bertie hurried to his
room and closed the door. He found
his old goldfish bowl – the one that
had belonged to his pet worm, Arthur,
before Mum threw him out – and filled
it with mud, leaves and a dollop of
peanut butter. Peanut butter was
Eugene's favourite.

Dirty Bertie

Bertie rushed downstairs. He found the *Marvo Book of 101 Magic Tricks* in the lounge and flicked through the pages. There were card tricks, vanishing tricks, mind-reading tricks … but not a single mention of worms. Bertie threw the book down in disgust. He was really starting to worry now. What if Eugene was stuck as a worm for ever? How was he going to explain it to Eugene's mum? She'd probably faint from the shock.

"BERTIE!"

Uh oh. Mum was calling.

"Bertie!" she yelled again. "Come here this minute!"

Bertie trailed into the kitchen. "What?"

"Don't pretend you don't know. What have I told you about keeping pets in your room?"

Dirty Bertie

Bertie turned pale. His mum was holding a goldfish bowl – an empty goldfish bowl.

"W-w-where is he?" he gasped.

"If you mean your revolting worm, I threw it out in the garden where it belongs."

"Nooooooooo!" wailed Bertie.

Dashing outside, Bertie searched the flower beds on all fours. Eugene might be anywhere by now. He could have crawled under a rock or been swallowed by a crow. And it would *all* be Bertie's fault. Eugene would never forgive him — especially if he was already dead. Bertie scrabbled around in the dirt. Out of the corner of his eye, he caught sight of something.

"Eugene!" Bertie had never been so relieved in his life. But wait a moment, there was more than one worm. There were three! Three fat pink worms — which was Eugene?

"Eugene?" said Bertie. "Speak to me! Wiggle your head if it's you!"

Dirty Bertie

The worms all wriggled, but not in a way that helped. It was no good. He would just have to keep all three until he could work out which one was Eugene. But where could he hide them? Not in his bedroom, Mum was bound to find them. It had to be somewhere she would never think to look. Bertie smiled to himself — he knew just the place.

DING DONG!

Bertie thumped downstairs and opened the door. Darren stood outside, grinning like mad.

"Hi, Bertie! Where's Eugene?" he asked.

"Shhh!" hissed Bertie. "Not so loud. He's safe upstairs."

"Really?" said Darren. "Are you sure?"

Dirty Bertie

"Of course I'm sure," said Bertie.

"Are you sure you're sure?"

"What is this? What's so funny?" asked Bertie.

"SUR-PRISE!"

Suddenly somebody leaped out from behind the door.

It was Eugene! He looked pretty calm for someone who'd recently been wriggling around in a flower bed. Bertie stared at him in astonishment. "But … but…"

"Ha ha! Your face! Hee hee!"

Eugene and Darren were laughing so much they could hardly speak.

"But how?" stammered Bertie. "You're a worm! I hid you upstairs!"

Darren wiped his eyes.

"Don't be stupid," he said. "We played a trick on you."

"A trick?"

"It was Darren's idea," explained Eugene. "We found a worm and put it in my jumper. I was hiding in the bushes watching the whole time."

"And you believed it!" giggled Darren. "You *actually* believed it."

"I didn't really," said Bertie.

"You did!" hooted Darren. "You were in such a panic."

Bertie laughed. He had to admit it had been a clever trick.

Dirty Bertie

"ARGGHHHHH!"

A deafening scream came from upstairs.

"What was that?" asked Eugene.

"That?" said Bertie. "That sounds like my sister. I think she might have found something in her drawer."

"BERTIE!" yelled Suzy.

"Come on," said Bertie. "I think it's time for a real magic trick. The one where I disappear!"